W9-CPM-942

Busytown Mysteries

With the timeless characters of RICHARD SCARRY

The Big Tooth Mystery

adapted by Natalie Shaw
based on the screenplay "The Big Tooth Mystery!"
written by Erika Strobel

Simon Spotlight

New York   London   Toronto   Sydney

SIMON SPOTLIGHT
An imprint of Simon & Schuster Children's Publishing Division
1230 Avenue of the Americas, New York, New York 10020
Busytown Mysteries™ and all related and associated trademarks are owned by Cookie Jar Entertainment Inc. and
used under license from Cookie Jar Entertainment Inc. © 2011 Cookie Jar Entertainment Inc. All Rights Reserved.
All rights reserved, including the right of reproduction in whole or in part in any form.
SIMON SPOTLIGHT and colophon are registered trademarks of Simon & Schuster, Inc.
For information about special discounts for bulk purchases, please contact Simon & Schuster Special Sales
at 1-866-506-1949 or business@simonandschuster.com.
Manufactured in the United States of America 1210 LAK
First Edition 10 9 8 7 6 5 4 3 2 1
ISBN 978-1-4424-1336-8

Huckle and Sally were driving past the Busytown Museum when they heard a loud whistle.

"Come to a full stop, please!" said Sergeant Murphy. He motioned for a big eighteen-wheeler truck to cross the intersection.

The big truck was carrying a dinosaur skeleton! Once it was parked in front of the museum, Sergeant Murphy waved the drivers through. Huckle and Sally quickly parked their vehicles and hopped out.

"Look at that *Tyrannosaurus rex* skeleton!" yelled Huckle. "It's as big as a house!"

"It's going to be in an exhibit at the Busytown Museum," said Sergeant Murphy, "but it almost didn't make it! Baker Humperdink accidentally hit the truck with his bread van on the way here. No one was hurt, but some of the bones fell off of the skeleton."

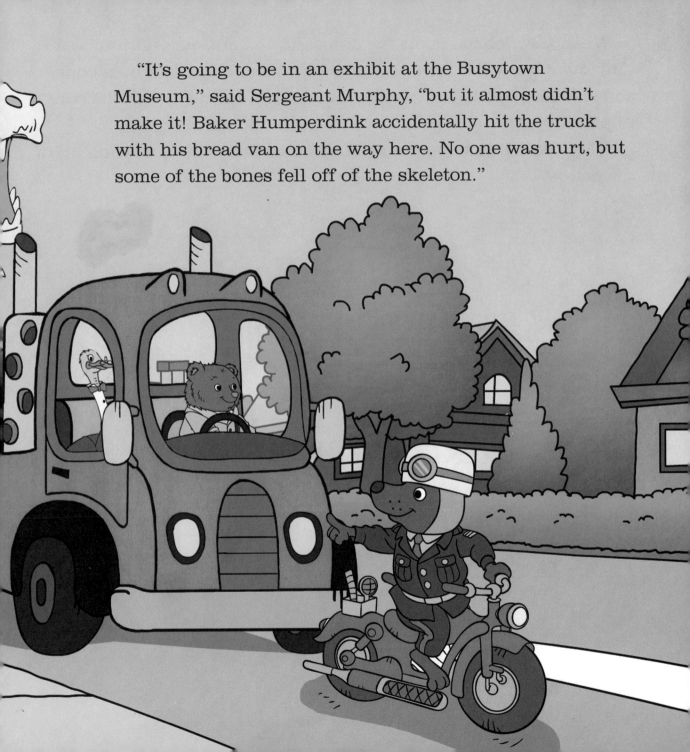

When they looked up at the dinosaur, the museum curator was already at work reattaching the loose bones. He picked up a bone, added a dab of glue, and used a long broom handle to put the bone in place.

"Gee, too bad Lowly's not around," said Sally. "He's missing all of the action."

"No, I'm not!" said the broom handle. It was Lowly Worm—in disguise! Everyone laughed as he hopped down to the ground. "I saw all of the action from up there. You might even say I was totally *glued* to it . . . get it? Say, all of this work has made me hungry. Who's up for a hot pretzel?"

"Great idea, Lowly," Sally said. "To the Busytown Bakery!"

They were about to enter the bakery when
Huckle spotted something.

"Hey, look at this," Huckle said. It was
yellow, very long, and pointy on one end.

"It kind of looks like a tooth," Sally said.
"A very *big* tooth."

"But why would a tooth just be lying on the road?" asked Lowly.
"And who could such a big tooth belong to?"
"I don't know," said Huckle, "but I do know
that this is a mystery!"

Toot, toot! Goldbug drove up in his news van. "Goldbug here, reporting live from the Busytown Bakery. What mystery are you sinking your teeth into today, Huckle?"

"Well, Goldbug," said Huckle, "I just found a giant tooth, and we're going to find out who it belongs to."

"Stay tuned as Huckle and his team chew things over. Goldbug, out!" He dropped back down into his van and zoomed away.

Pig Will trotted past, wearing the head of a dinosaur costume, and growled just like a dinosaur. Then his tail growled too! Pig Will turned to his tail and said, "Pig Won't, dinosaur tails don't growl!" Pig Won't started to wag his tail instead, which made everyone laugh.

"Hey, why are you dressed up like a dinosaur?" asked Huckle. The pigs said they were passing out free tickets to the Busytown Museum, and they gave three tickets to Huckle.

The gang thanked the brothers for the tickets. Huckle asked Sally and Lowly if they had any ideas about how to solve the mystery.

"Well, since it's a big tooth, it probably came from someone *really* big," said Sally. "Let's ask Hilda Hippo if she lost a tooth!"

Hilda Hippo opened her mouth wide as Huckle held the tooth up. "Nope, it's not a match. Your teeth are small and round, not big and pointy like this one."

They stopped by the ice-cream shop to see if Ellie Elephant might have lost a tooth. While Ellie's teeth were big, they were smaller than the mystery tooth. They weren't sharp and pointy either.

"Also your teeth are nice and white, not brownish yellow," said Sally.

Next they tracked down Jeremy Giraffe. He was very tall, but his teeth were square and small. It seemed like no one in Busytown had teeth the same size, shape, and color as their mystery tooth.

"Maybe we need to talk to someone who's an expert on teeth," suggested Lowly. "I bet Dr. Dentist could help us figure out who this tooth belongs to!"

Dr. Dentist examined the giant tooth carefully. "Hmmm. I've never seen a tooth like this before, but judging by its size, you were right to think that it belongs to someone very big . . . who has never, *ever* brushed his or her teeth!"

They thanked Dr. Dentist and headed outside.
"Maybe that's why this tooth fell out!" said
Sally. "Whoever it belongs to never brushed it!"
"Ewww!" said Lowly. "Look, there's Baker
Humperdink's bread van!"

"Hi, Baker Humperdink! We heard about your accident this morning," said Sally. "Are you all right?"

"I'm fine, but I hear that dinosaur lost some bones," said Baker Humperdink. "I sure hope the museum found them."

Huckle looked at the tooth in his hand, then to the dinosaur poster, and grinned. "That's it! I think I know whose tooth this is! To the museum!"

Everyone looked up at the big dinosaur, and Goldbug asked Huckle if he'd solved the mystery.

"I think so, Goldbug," said Huckle. "When Baker Humperdink's truck knocked some of the dinosaur bones loose, I think it also knocked a tooth loose."

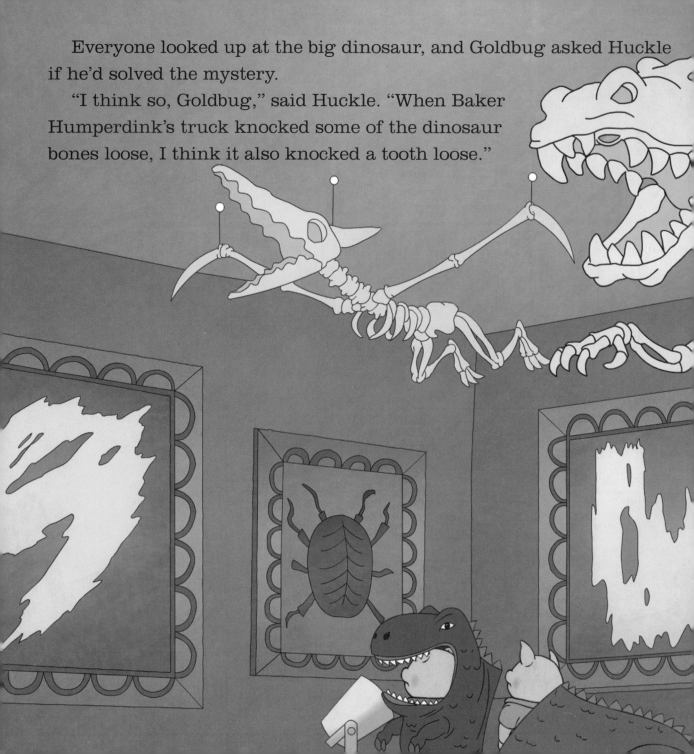

"Huckle's right!" said Sally. "The *Tyrannosaurus rex* is missing a tooth!"

The museum curator rushed into the room. "Thank goodness—you found the tooth! It's millions of years old, you know!"

"Wow! That's a really long time to go without brushing your teeth!" said Lowly.

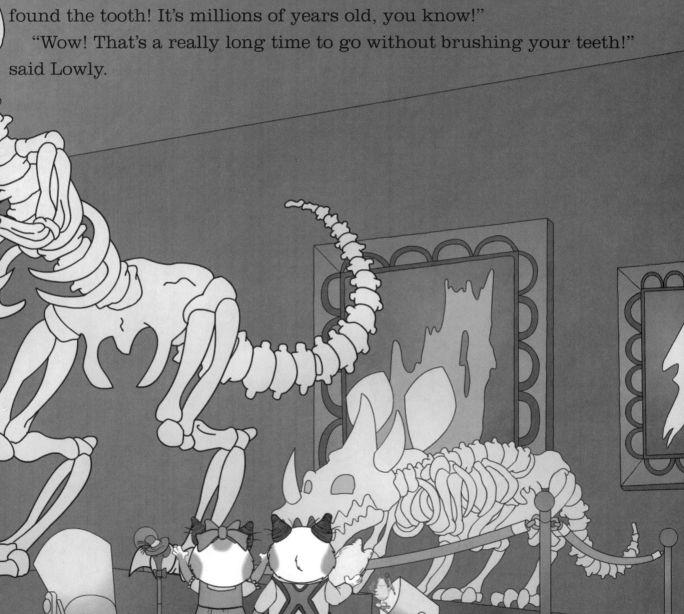

"Well, there you have it!" said Goldbug. "Huckle has solved the mystery!"

"Hurray for Huckle!" everyone cheered. They spent the rest of the afternoon at the very busy Busytown Museum learning all about dinosaurs.